The Little Squeegy Bug

By Bill Martin Jr and Michael Sampson

Illustrated by Patrick Corrigan

Marshall Cavendish Children

Once upon a time there was a little squeegy bug. No one knew where he came from. He wasn't an ant. He wasn't a cricket. And he certainly wasn't a flea.

One day the little squeegy bug was down by the brook watching the sunbeams play hopscotch on the water. Then, Z-z-z-z-z, a big bumblebee flew down from the sky. He made so much noise that the grass trembled and all the little bugs were frightened. But not the squeegy bug. He was not one bit afraid. Looking up at the bumblebee, he asked,

"Who are you?"

"I'm Buzzer the Bumblebee. I carry a stinger in my tail."

"Oh," said the squeegy bug, "I'd like to be a bumblebee and carry a stinger in my tail, too."

"You could never be a bumblebee
without silver wings like mine."
    "Where can I get silver wings
like yours?"
    "You'll have to climb to the sky,"
buzzed the bumblebee.

"To the sky?" thought the little squeegy bug. "Maybe I *could* climb to the sky."

The little squeegy

bug found the tallest cattail that grew by the brook.

He looked up. The cattail seemed so high that he thought surely it touched the sky. He started climbing. For three days and three nights the little bug climbed and climbed and climbed. Finally, he stopped to rest. He looked down. But he was up so high he couldn't see the ground. He closed his eyes and climbed faster and faster, until at last he came to the top of the cattail.

Just then, a big black storm cloud came out of the west, and the lamp in the moon went out. Thunder crashed. Lightning flashed. And the rain pelted down so hard that the little squeegy bug was afraid he'd be washed away and he'd never find his silver wings.

Now there lived in the cattail leaf an old caterpillar. His name was Creepy. He heard the little squeegy bug crying so he crawled out of bed, lit his lantern, and peered up into the darkness. "What's the matter up there?" he called.

"I'm a little squeegy bug. I'm trying to find the sky, but the sky is falling apart."

"You must be a stranger," said the old caterpillar.

"Anyone who lives on the cattail knows this is only a summer storm. Come with me. I'll take you home for tonight."

So the little squeegy
bug and the old caterpillar
walked down the cattail leaf
to the caterpillar's home.
They went to bed and slept
soundly until morning.

As soon as the sun was up, they went out on the cattail leaf in search of the sky. The old caterpillar didn't know the way. "But," he said, "I have a friend who can tell us. His name is Haunchy the Spider. He lives in a castle of webs at the end of the cattail leaf."

So they walked to the end of the

cattail leaf to the castle of webs and knocked on the door.

The door opened, and there stood a tiny little
spider with more feet than he knew what to do
with. "Good morning, Haunchy the Spider," said the
little squeegy bug. "Can you help me find the sky?"

The spider asked, "Why do you want to go
to the sky?"

"Buzzer the Bumblebee said if I could climb to
the sky, I could find some silver wings. Then I would
be a bumblebee and carry a stinger in my tail."

"I think Buzzer the Bumblebee was teasing you,"
said Haunchy the Spider. "But come with me, I'll
help you find your silver wings."

They walked to

the top of the cattail.

Haunchy the Spider pulled out his spinning wheel and started to spin silver threads to make a pair of silver wings.

Then he shaped the silver threads into a pair of beautiful wings. He lifted them carefully and placed them on the squeegy bug's back. The little bug was so excited that he flapped his wings. He was ready to fly away, but he stopped.

"What's the matter?" called Haunchy the Spider.

"I don't have a stinger in my tail,"
said the little squeegy bug.
"You weren't meant to have a stinger
in your tail. You're not a bumblebee.
You're just a little squeegy bug without
a name. So I will give you a name."

Haunchy the Spider reached up
into the sky and took the brightest
star he could find. He hung that star
in the squeegy bug's tail.

"Here, little squeegy bug, here's a lantern to carry in your tail," said Haunchy the Spider. "It's better than a stinger. Stingers hurt people. But with your light you can help people. You can light the way through the night for everyone in the world. You shall be called Squeegy the Firefly, the Lamplighter of the Sky."

The squeegy bug was very happy. At
last he had his silver wings, a lantern to
carry in his tail, and, best of all, a name.
He thanked his friends for helping him
and flew up, up, up, past sun and moon

and stars.

And wherever he went, his lantern shone brightly

in the night sky.

To my brother Bernard, who made the first squeegy bug fly.
B.M. Jr

To my sister Patsy, for the songs she sang to me.
M.S.

Dedicated to Roland Patenaude.
P.C.

Text copyright © 2001 by Bill Martin, Jr and Michael Sampson
Illustration copyright © 2001 by Patrick Corrigan

Marshall Cavendish Corporation, 99 White Plains Road, Tarrytown, NY 10591
www.marshallcavendish.us

Library of Congress Cataloging-in-Publication Data
Martin, Bill, 1916-
The little squeegy bug / by Bill Martin, Jr. and Michael Sampson; illustrated by Patrick Corrigan.
p. cm.
Summary: A wingless little bug with no name wants to be a bumblebee and begins to search for a pair of wings.
ISBN-13: 978-0-7614-5243-0
ISBN-10: 0-7614-5243-5 (pbk.)
[1. Insects—Fiction. 2. Individuality—Fiction. 3. Wings—Fiction. 4. Fireflies—Fiction.] I. Sampson, Michael R. II.
Corrigan, Pat (Patrick B.), ill. III. Title
2004058623

The Little Squeegy Bug was self-published in a longer version, with illustrations by Bernard Martin, in 1945.

Creative director: Bretton Clark
Designer: Billy Kelly
Editor: Margery Cuyler
Calligraphy by John Stevens

The illustrations in this book were prepared digitally.

Printed in China

First Marshall Cavendish paperback edition, 2005
Reprinted by arrangement with WinslowHouse International, Inc.

4 6 8 10 9 7 5 3

mc Marshall Cavendish
Children